STARS OF SPORTS

ELENA DELLE DONNE

BASKETBALL RECORD BREAKER

by Matt Chandler

CAPSTONE PRESS
a capstone imprint

Published by Capstone Press, an imprint of Capstone
1710 Roe Crest Drive, North Mankato, Minnesota 56003
capstonepub.com

Copyright © 2023 by Capstone. All rights reserved. No part of this publication may be reproduced in whole or in part, or stored in a retrieval system, or transmitted in any form or by any means, electronic, mechanical, photocopying, recording, or otherwise, without written permission of the publisher.

SPORTS ILLUSTRATED KIDS is a trademark of ABG-SI LLC. Used with permission.

Library of Congress Cataloging-in-Publication Data is available on the Library of Congress website.
ISBN: 9781666352603 (hardcover)
ISBN: 9781666352610 (ebook PDF)

Summary: Elena Delle Donne made her WNBA debut in 2013 and earned the Rookie of the Year award. It was just a glimpse of what was to come. Delle Donne has been an All-Star six times, and she led the Washington Mystics to a championship win in 2019. Get the highlights of Delle Donne's amazing career.

Editorial Credits
Editor: Carrie Sheely; Designer: Bobbie Nuytten; Media Researcher: Morgan Walters; Production Specialist: Polly Fisher

Image Credits
Associated Press: Kamil Krzaczynski, 25, MediaPunch, 7, Nick Wass, Cover, 5, 28, Rob Carr, 19; Getty Images: Jonathan Daniel, 15, The Washington Post, 9; Newscom: Anthony Nesmith/Cal Sport Media, 23, Ben Smidt/Icon SMI 295, 17; Shutterstock: Oleksii Sidorov, 1; Sports Illustrated: Al Tielemans, 21, Erick W. Rasco, 11, 24, 27; Wikimedia: Dannykuconn, 13

Source Notes
Pg. 6, "I said I . . . " "Delle Donne on Battling Lyme Disease and Her Biggest Inspiration," ESPN The Magazine, Body Issue 2016, July 5, 2016.
Pg. 8, "When I think . . . " "A World Class Basketball Player and a World Class Role Model, " Elena Delle Donne Official Staff in Advocacy, January 4, 2016, https://elenadelledonne.com/a-world-class-basketball-player-and-a-world-class-role-model/
Pg. 8, "Lizzie doesn't know . . . " "Elena Delle Donne on Becoming Sister Lizzie's Caretaker: 'She'll Be With Me,'" The News Journal, May 21, 2019, https://www.delawareonline.com/story/life/2019/05/21/elena-delle-donne-becoming-sister-lizzies-caretaker-shell-me/3751079002/
Pg. 15, "Kids would be . . . ." "Delle Donne on Battling Lyme Disease and Her Biggest Inspiration," ESPN The Magazine, Body Issue 2016, July 5, 2016.
Pg. 16, "I always felt . . . " "The Audacity of Height," ESPN, November 22, 2016, https://www.espn.com/espn/feature/story/_/page/espnw-delledonne161122/chicago-sky-elena-delle-donne-spent-years-learning-accept-height
Pg. 20, "We fought . . . " "Women's Basketball Sweet 16 vs. Kentucky Press Conference," Delaware Blue Hens, March 30, 2013, https://www.youtube.com/watch?v=RtrfZFuJwC8
All websites accessed November 2021

All internet sites appearing in back matter were available and accurate when this book was sent to press.

TABLE OF CONTENTS

WNBA CHAMPION 4

CHAPTER 1
FAMILY FIRST 6

CHAPTER 2
A STAR IS BORN 10

CHAPTER 3
OFF TO COLLEGE 16

CHAPTER 4
CHICAGO SUPERSTAR 22

CHAPTER 5
DELLE DONNE DELIVERS 26

TIMELINE 29
GLOSSARY 30
READ MORE 31
INTERNET SITES 31
INDEX 32

Words in **BOLD** are in the glossary.

WNBA CHAMPION

It was Game 5 of the 2019 WNBA Finals. The Washington Mystics were playing the Connecticut Sun. The winning team would be the WNBA champions.

The Mystics' star player Elena Delle Donne was hurt. She had a broken nose that required her to wear a face guard. She also suffered from a painful back injury. Still, she took to the court in the biggest game of the season.

The center scored 21 points despite her injuries. She managed nine rebounds and added two **assists**. It wasn't her best performance of the season. But it was enough to lead her team to victory. The Mystics defeated the Sun 89–78. Delle Donne was a WNBA Champion!

>>> Elena Delle Donne takes a jump shot during Game 5 of the 2019 WNBA Finals.

CHAPTER 1
FAMILY FIRST

Elena Delle Donne was born in Wilmington, Delaware, on September 5, 1989. Her family includes her parents Joan and Ernest and a brother and sister. Her older brother, Gene, was also an athlete, playing college basketball and football. Delle Donne played backyard basketball with her big brother. She wanted to be a basketball player when she was a little girl. "I said I wanted to be the best female basketball player in the world when I was 4," Delle Donne said in a 2016 interview. "I've always had really lofty goals."

By the time she was 3 years old, Delle Donne was so tall people thought she was in elementary school. Her doctor even wanted to give her medicine to slow her growth. Her parents said no, and they taught Delle Donne to love her height.

>>> Delle Donne's parents, Joan and Ernest, watch her play in a 2016 game.

SISTERLY LOVE

Delle Donne's older sister, Lizzie, was born blind and deaf. She also has **autism** and **cerebral palsy**. The two sisters are very close. Delle Donne calls Lizzie her biggest inspiration. When Delle Donne is injured or battling sickness, she refuses to give up.

"When I think about how tired I am or how much it hurts—I think about Lizzie," Delle Donne once wrote. "She inspires me. None of my hardships are even close to the same plane as what she has endured."

Many WNBA players earn millions of dollars playing in overseas leagues during the WNBA off-season. Delle Donne has turned down many offers to play overseas because she doesn't want to be too far away from Lizzie. "Lizzie doesn't know that I play basketball . . . " Delle Donne said. "She just knows that I am one of her people and a really important person in her life. And that's all I want to be."

>>> Spending time at her parents' property allows Delle Donne to be close to her family.

CHAPTER 2
A STAR IS BORN

Delle Donne's height made her a natural fit for basketball. But it is her hard work as a child that her parents and coaches talk about.

Growing up, Delle Donne says her brother had a personal trainer. One day she asked to join them for a basketball workout. The trainer helped Delle Donne learn the game. Today, as a WNBA superstar, she still works with the same trainer from her childhood.

Delle Donne was driven to be the best basketball player she could be. She was determined to be seen as more than just a tall girl. She became so good that when she was seven, she was playing on a boys' team with 11-year-olds.

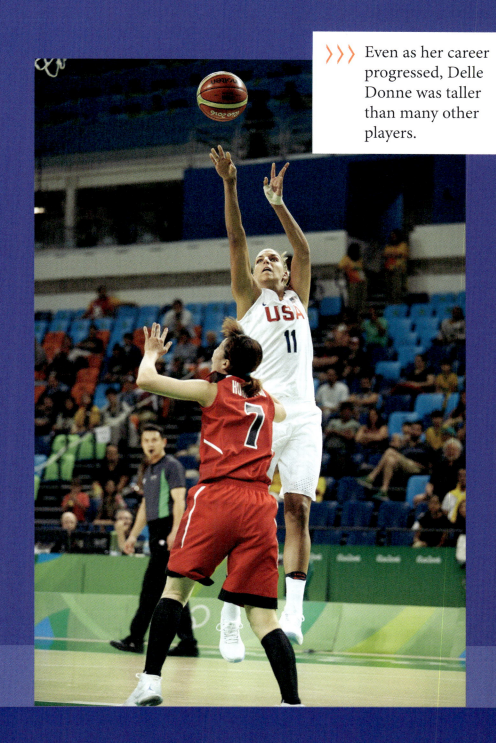

>>> Even as her career progressed, Delle Donne was taller than many other players.

By sixth grade, Delle Donne was over 6 feet (183 centimeters) tall. Though she was good enough, she wasn't allowed to play high school basketball until she reached eighth grade.

Instead, Delle Donne advanced her skills by playing basketball in an Amateur Athletic Union (AAU) league. She won three championships as a member of Fencor, an AAU team in nearby Pennsylvania.

When she was in eighth grade, Delle Donne began attending high school at Ursuline Academy. The school was close to her home in Delaware. It also had a very good basketball program. Delle Donne was a star on her new team. She averaged more than 20 points per game. Led by Delle Donne, Ursuline Academy won the state championship in her first season on the team.

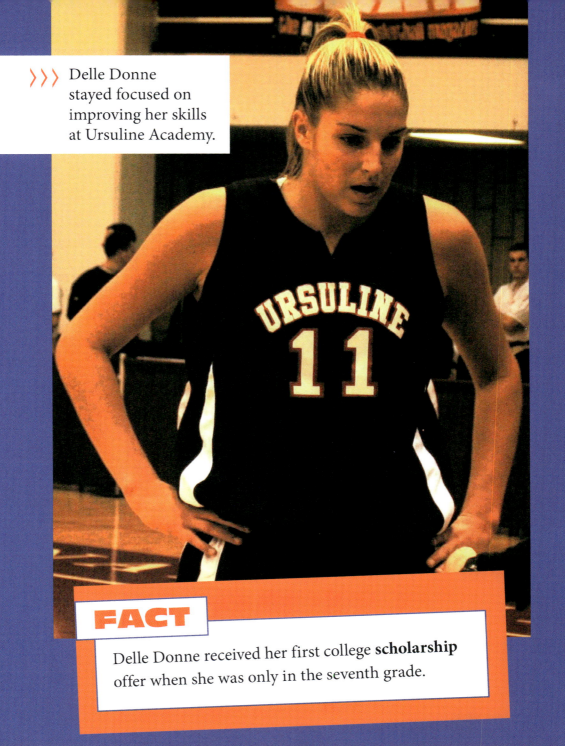

>>> Delle Donne stayed focused on improving her skills at Ursuline Academy.

FACT

Delle Donne received her first college **scholarship** offer when she was only in the seventh grade.

HIGH SCHOOL HERO

Delle Donne became a legend at Ursuline Academy. After her amazing eighth-grade season, she led the team to three state championships in a row. By her senior year, Delle Donne averaged more than 30 points and 11 rebounds per game. She finished her career at Ursuline with 2,818 points scored. That was the record for most points scored by a high school basketball player in the history of Delaware.

Delle Donne was also named the Gatorade Player of the Year for Delaware three times during her high school career. It was one of more than a dozen awards the teenager collected during high school.

FACT

In high school, Delle Donne once made 80 straight free throws!

Delle Donne's top-level play in high school earned her a position on the McDonald's All American team in 2008.

Mom Knows Best

Delle Donne's height as a child was sometimes hard for her. Some kids would say things about her height.

"Kids would be like, '. . . you're taller than my dad. Oh, you look like a monster!'" she recalled. During those tough times, her mom helped her through. "She would always tell me how unique I am and say, 'Why try to be like the rest of the pack? Be your own person,'" Delle Donne told ESPN in an interview. Those words and the love of her family helped Delle Donne feel comfortable with her body.

CHAPTER 3
OFF TO COLLEGE

Many top colleges **recruited** Delle Donne to play for them. In her senior year of high school, she chose the University of Connecticut (UConn). But after just two days there, Delle Donne left. She missed her family, especially Lizzie. Worst of all, she didn't want to play basketball anymore.

Delle Donne switched schools and enrolled at the University of Delaware, the school closest to her home. Still, she didn't want to play basketball. Instead, she joined the school's volleyball team. At the time, Delle Donne wasn't sure she would ever play basketball again. "I always felt like I was kind of following the path everybody told me to go," she said. "I think that's why I went through . . . what I did, because finally I was like, . . . Do I really want to do this, or do I want to be something else?"

>>> Delle Donne's success on the court in high school led to opportunities to attend and play basketball at several colleges.

BACK ON THE COURT

On November 17, 2009, Delle Donne made her return to the game of basketball. Twenty months after she played her last high school game, she suited up for the Delaware Blue Hens. Delle Donne missed playing basketball. She missed the competition. Playing in Delaware also meant staying close to her family. All that drove her to return to the game she once said she had grown to dislike.

Delle Donne didn't miss a beat in her **debut**. She led all scorers with 19 points. She added seven rebounds and five assists to lead her team to a 77–64 win.

During her sophomore season, Delle Donne missed several games after becoming ill. It would take until her junior year to show the strong play she displayed at Ursuline.

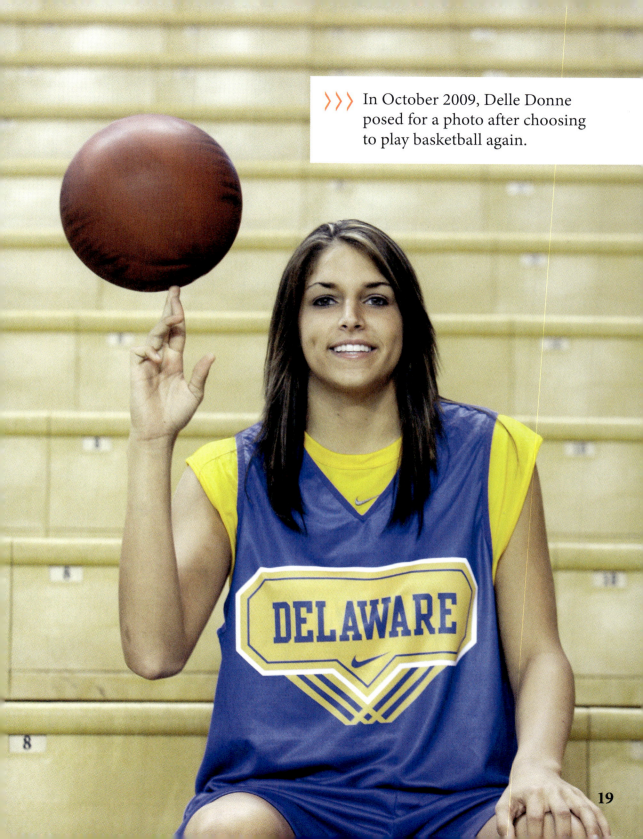

In October 2009, Delle Donne posed for a photo after choosing to play basketball again.

READY FOR THE WNBA

Delle Donne led the nation in scoring her junior season, averaging more than 28 points per game. She led the Blue Hens to a perfect 18–0 record.

Delle Donne topped off her college career by leading Delaware to the Sweet 16 of the 2013 NCAA Tournament. Facing Kentucky, she delivered 33 points. Delaware lost the game, but Delle Donne remained positive. "We fought to the very end, and I'm just very proud of everyone," she said after the game. "We made a lot of history in Delaware, and I think we made our fans very proud."

Lyme Disease Battle

Delle Donne has been battling Lyme disease since 2008. The disease causes tiredness, flu-like symptoms, and sore muscles. Delle Donne's battle with the illness is ongoing. In 2020, Delle Donne said she took 64 pills every day to treat the symptoms and stay healthy enough to play basketball. That is unusual. Most people with Lyme disease get better in just a few weeks after they get sick.

>>> Delle Donne passes to a Delaware teammate during a 2012 game.

CHAPTER 4
CHICAGO SUPERSTAR

On April 15, 2013, Delle Donne's dream came true. The Chicago Sky selected her with the second overall pick in the WNBA Draft. The girl who had dreamed of playing professional basketball had made it!

Delle Donne became an instant superstar in Chicago. She led the team in scoring, averaging more than 18 points per game in her **rookie** season. Her biggest offensive night came in August at home against the Minnesota Lynx. Delle Donne scored a season high of 32 points. She added six rebounds and four blocks to lead the Sky to a 94–86 overtime win.

The Sky finished the 2013 season with the best record in the Eastern Conference. Delle Donne was the **unanimous** choice for WNBA Rookie of the Year.

>>> Delle Donne takes a shot over Connecticut Sun guard Allison Hightower in a game on July 12, 2013.

WASHINGTON MYSTICS

Delle Donne's success continued with the Chicago Sky over the next several seasons. She led the Sky to the 2014 WNBA Finals. She had a standout season in 2015. She finished the season as the Sky's single-season leader in scoring with 725 points. She even won an Olympic gold medal in 2016 as a member of Team USA.

>>> Delle Donne (left) and some of her teammates pose with their gold medals at the 2016 Summer Olympics.

Although Delle Donne had plenty of success, she wanted to play closer to home. She threatened to sit out the 2017 season unless the Sky traded her. On February 2, 2017, she got her wish. Delle Donne was traded to the Washington Mystics.

Before Delle Donne, the Mystics had only four winning seasons in their 19 years of existence. In her first three seasons in Washington, the franchise had winning records and played in two WNBA Finals.

League MVP

The highlight of Delle Donne's time in Chicago was winning the 2015 league MVP Award. Delle Donne led the league in scoring with 23.4 points per game. She also had a free throw percentage of .950.

CHAPTER 5
DELLE DONNE DELIVERS

After being swept in the 2018 WNBA Finals, the pressure was on Delle Donne. The expectations were high for 2019. Superstars often play their best when the pressure is on. Delle Donne delivered. She stayed healthy and played in 31 of her team's 34 regular-season games. She led the Mystics in points and rebounds, scoring more than 600 points. Thanks to Delle Donne's incredible play, the Mystics finished the season 26–8. It was the best record in the WNBA.

In the playoffs, Delle Donne was unstoppable, even though she was battling knee and back injuries. She led the Mystics to a 3–1 series win over the Las Vegas Aces to advance to the WNBA Finals. She then led the Mystics to a series win against the Connecticut Sun. The team had its first-ever WNBA title!

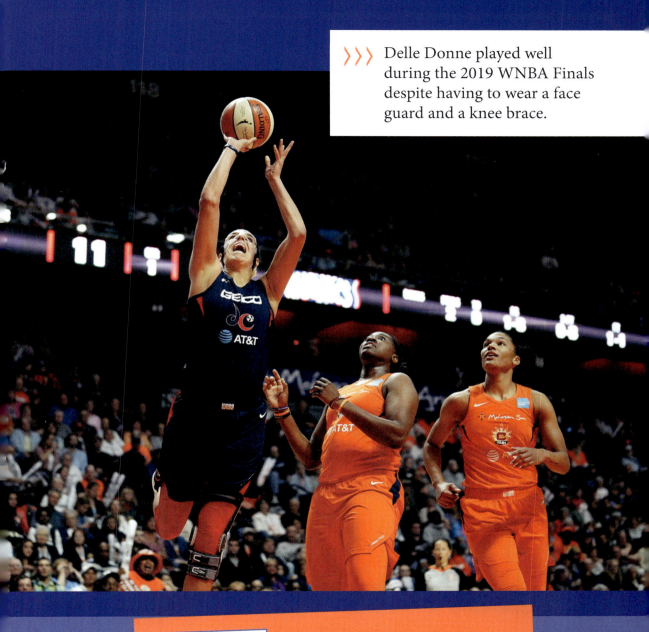

››› Delle Donne played well during the 2019 WNBA Finals despite having to wear a face guard and a knee brace.

FACT

Delle Donne tied a WNBA record by making 59 consecutive free throws in a one-season time period in 2017.

THE FUTURE AWAITS

Delle Donne sat out the 2020 season. She didn't want to risk getting sick from COVID-19. She played only three games in 2021 due to injury.

Delle Donne is in her 30s. She has battled some serious injuries as well as Lyme disease. Yet she keeps herself in excellent physical shape. She is a two-time league MVP, a WNBA champion, and an Olympian. Her family has always been her top priority. But many WNBA fans hope the superstar has several seasons left of top-level basketball to play!

››› Delle Donne walks off the court after a playoff game in 2018.

TIMELINE

1989 — Elena Delle Donne is born in Wilmington, Delaware, on September 5.

2004 — Delle Donne leads Ursuline Academy to the state championship when she is in eighth grade.

2006 — Delle Donne sets the national high school record, making 80 consecutive free throws.

2013 — Delle Donne is named WNBA Rookie of the Year.

2015 — After leading the WNBA in scoring, Delle Donne wins her first WNBA MVP Award.

2016 — Delle Donne wins an Olympic gold medal as a member of Team USA.

2017 — The Chicago Sky trade Delle Donne to the Washington Mystics.

2019 — Delle Donne is named to her sixth WNBA All-Star team.

2019 — Delle Donne wins her first WNBA Championship.

2020 — Due to health concerns because of COVID-19, Delle Donne sits out the 2020 season.

GLOSSARY

ASSIST (uh-SIST)—a pass that leads to a score by a teammate

AUTISM (AW-tiss-uhm)—a condition that causes people to have trouble communicating and forming relationships with others; they may have difficulty with language

CEREBRAL PALSY (se-REE-brul POL-zee)—a brain disorder that affects a person's ability to move and maintain balance

DEBUT (DAY-byoo)—a player's first game

RECRUIT (ri-KROOT)—to ask someone to join a company or organization

ROOKIE (RUK-ee)—a first-year player

SCHOLARSHIP (SKOL-ur-ship)—money given to a student to pay for school

UNANIMOUS (yoo-NAN-uh-muhss)—agreed on by everyone

READ MORE

Buckey, A.W. *Women in Basketball*. Lake Elmo, MN: Focus Readers, 2020.

Chandler, Matt. *On the Court: Biographies of Today's Best Basketball Players*. Emeryville, CA: Rockridge Press, 2020.

Labrecque, Ellen. *The Story of the WNBA*. North Mankato, MN: The Child's World, 2020.

Omoth, Tyler. *The WNBA Finals*. North Mankato, MN: Capstone, 2020.

INTERNET SITES

ESPN: Finding Her Way Back Home
espn.com/espn/eticket/story?page=elenaDonne

Official Website of Elena Delle Donne
elenadelledonne.com

WNBA: Elena Delle Donne
wnba.com/player/elena-delle-donne/

INDEX

Amateur Athletic Union (AAU), 12

assists, 4, 18

blocks, 22

Chicago Sky, 22, 24, 25

Delaware Blue Hens, 18, 20

Delle Donne, Lizzie, 8, 16

Eastern Conference, 22

free throws, 14, 25, 27

Gatorade Player of the Year, 14

Lyme disease, 20, 28

MVP Award, 25, 28

points, 4, 12, 14, 18, 20, 22, 24, 25, 26

rebounds, 4, 14, 18, 22, 26

Rookie of the Year, 22

scholarships, 13

University of Delaware, 16, 18, 20

Ursuline Academy, 12, 13, 14, 18

Washington Mystics, 4, 24, 25, 26

WNBA Finals, 4, 5, 24, 25, 26, 27

AUTHOR BIO

Matt Chandler is the author of more than 60 books for children and thousands of articles published in newspapers and magazines. He writes mostly nonfiction books with a focus on sports, ghosts and haunted places, and graphic novels. Matt lives in New York.